TRAFFIC JAM

Also by Annie Owen

Annie's abc
Annie's One to Ten

TRAFFIC JAM

pop!
chugga
ding-a-ling
fssss
fsssssss
taooooot!

Annie Owen

ORCHARD BOOKS

For Rufus, with love

Text and illustrations © Annie Owen 1990
First published in Great Britain in 1990 by
ORCHARD BOOKS
96 Leonard Street, London EC2A 4RH
Orchard Books Australia
14 Mars Road, Lane Cove NSW 2066
1 85213 159 4
A CIP catalogue record for this book
is available from the British Library.
Printed in Belgium

Can you see the bright blue car? Can you see the children? Off they go to the party. The road is busy but they've left plenty of time in case they get stuck in a traffic jam.

What can you see on the road?

Peepar! Peepar! a police car is chasing a red sports car. Drrmm-drrmm-drrmm, that's Sydney's school bus. And there's an ice-cream van,

the Bluebeard Seafood Restaurant van, a
squeaky bicycle, a farm truck, the Gold Rush
Butter pantechnicon, the bright blue car . . .

What else can you see?

Emergency! Weeeoooweeeooo! Fire engines
and a police car dash along, past Flossie's
flower van, the big Pitt's Parts delivery van,

a car driven by a clown, a car with a trailer, Billy Bowles's truck with a big load of bales, the bright blue car . . .

What else can you see?

Clank! Clank! That red car's broken down. But the little red truck keeps rattling along while the big limousine purrs past.

There's a giraffe in an animal bus! And look,
the green car's got a puncture and the bright
blue car goes vroom.

What else can you see?

Brrmm! Brrmm! The juggernauts roll along –
one pantechnicon full of Yum-Yum sweets
and another full of slippers, a water tanker,

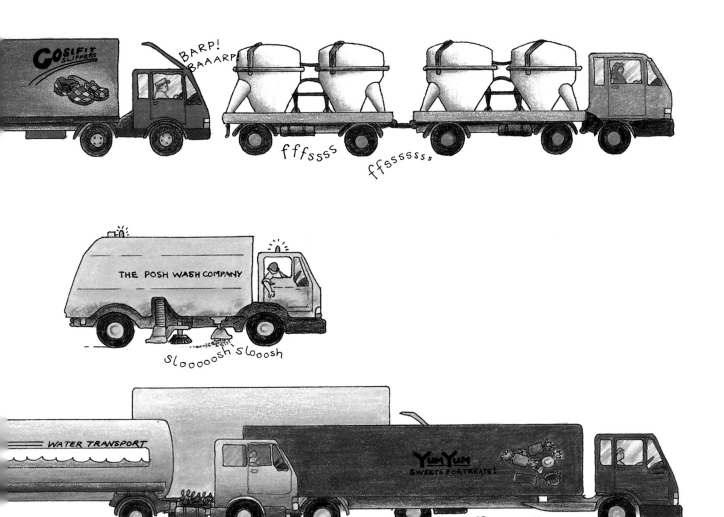

an oil tanker, and a car transporter with six cars.
The Posh Wash cleaner slooshes along the road
and the bright blue car goes toot! toot!

What else can you see?

Stop! Stop! There's been an accident! Squeak,
goes the hoist on the breakdown truck. The
green car's had a bash and so has Mr. Kidd's
orange van and the back of Freda's taxi.

Look what's stuck in the traffic – a builder's truck, the Star Glazing delivery van, a white sports car, a motorcycle, the bright blue car . . .

What else can you see?

Toot! Toot! Beep! Beep! Watch out for the
sheep! There's a tractor in the way. The green
car's had to stop and so has the waterbed van.

The green sports car's still going too fast, but the little jeep missed all the sheep and so has the bright blue car.

What else can you see?

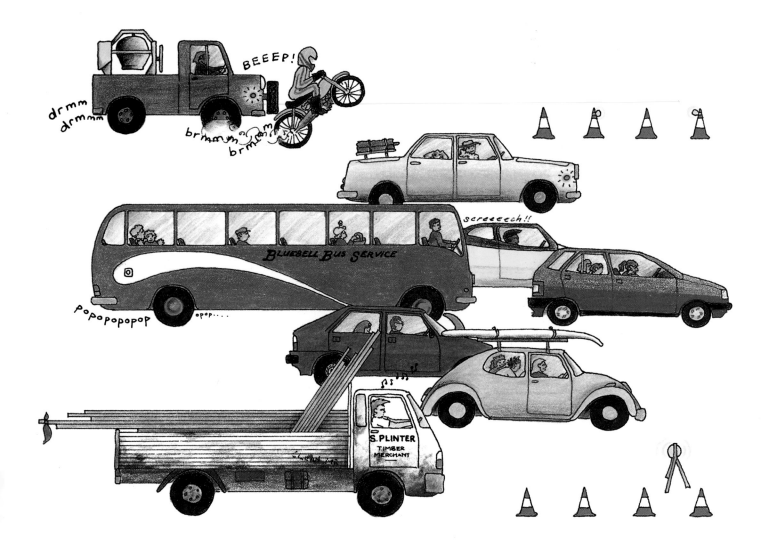

The road's up! And look what's come to mend it
– a yellow steamroller, a big orange digger and a
dump truck that goes dugga-dugga.

And there's a big black limousine on its way to
a wedding, a Bluebell bus pop-pop-popping
along, the bright blue car . . .

What else can you see?

Ting-a-ling! A bicycle race! Can you count the
bikes? And a cement mix truck phut-phuts along
behind a gardener's van with a trailer.

And there's Trevor's truck, Molly's milk float
and an ambulance, a tandem behind a white
mini-bus, the bright blue car . . .

                                             What else can you see?

Here comes the carnival parade! Chug-chug goes
the truck with the clowns on the back and the
truck with the carnival queen.

Ding-ding goes the articulated bus. And
there's that car with the clown again and Jasmin's
bread delivery van, the bright blue car . . .

What else can you see?

At last! The bright blue car has reached the end of its journey. And the children are just in time for the party.

THE AMAZING ADVENTURES OF

HANUMAN

Told by Rani and Jugnu Singh ❁ Illustrations by Biman Mullick

BBC BOOKS

HOW HANUMAN GOT HIS MAGIC POWERS

Once upon a time, long ago, there lived in India a monkey-boy called Hanuman. His father was Vayu, the god of the winds, and his mother was a monkey princess. Although he was only little, Hanuman had magic powers. He was also very naughty.

This is the story of some exciting adventures which began in the beautiful valley of flowers, where one day Hanuman sat with his mother in the warm sunshine.

Hanuman looked up into the sky and saw the sun.

'I like the sun,' said the naughty monkey-boy.

'How beautiful it is, so warm, so golden and so bright. I'd love to hold it and play with it as if it were my very own!'

He reached up, caught hold of the sun and started throwing it up and down as though it were a ball. The sun was not pleased, and began to feel rather ill.

The sun called out to Indra, the god of thunder and lightning, who was riding by on his magic elephant.

'Help! Indra! Look at what this naughty monkey-boy is doing to me! Help!'

Indra was very cross with Hanuman.

The sky grew dark and storm clouds gathered.

'Put the sun back at once,' he said in a mighty voice.

'NO,' said Hanuman, who was not afraid.

In fury Indra shot a bolt of white lightning.

'Zaap!'

It hit the monkey-boy.

Hanuman fell to the ground, where he lay very still. His father Vayu, who was flying over the earth, had a feeling that Hanuman was in danger. He rushed back to the valley of flowers and found his little son lying with his eyes closed.

'Who has done this to my son?' he called out from the sky. The god of the winds was furious and blew great winds and storms around the world. Then, all of a sudden, the air became still.

'I will stop the air from flowing everywhere until my son Hanuman breathes again!', said Vayu.

Now this was very serious for the world. Plants, animals and people quickly began to feel weak, fall over and die. They did not have any air to breathe. When Indra, the god of thunder and lightning, flew by and saw what was happening, he felt very sad for the world.

'Anger is such a terrible thing,' he said. 'None of this would have happened if I hadn't got so cross. I must ask Vayu to forgive me.'

Meanwhile Vayu had taken his son Hanuman deep under the ground and was cradling him in his arms. Indra called some other gods to beg Vayu to bring air back to the world.

'Not until Hanuman breathes again,' replied Vayu.

So the gods promised to bring the monkey-boy back to life and said that when he grew up he would have more magic powers. He could grow as big or as small as he wished. His tail would be magic and he could fly high in the sky. He would lead an army of monkeys and even live for as long as he liked!

'Lightning and thunder bolts will never harm him again,' said Indra.

'Fire will never touch him,' said the sun.

Hanuman's father was happy now and he kept his word. The air moved again and all the plants, animals and people came back to life.

'What happened to us?' they asked. They couldn't remember anything!

Everything took place as the gods promised. Hanuman grew up to be the most fantastic monkey in the world. He lived in an enormous green forest. Sugreeva, the king of monkeys, heard about Hanuman's special powers. He went to see him.

'Will you be my best friend and lead my army?' Sugreeva asked.

'Certainly,' said Hanuman, and from that day on the two were always together.

THE KIDNAPPING OF SITA

At the other end of the forest lived a handsome prince called Rama and his beautiful, clever wife princess Sita. The news of her beauty spread far and wide. Now, down at the southern tip of India, on an island called Lanka, there lived a wicked, jealous demon with ten heads and twenty arms. His name was Ravana.

'I will make Sita my wife,' he boasted, 'even if I have to steal her!' He sent his wicked demons, disguised as golden deer, to lure prince Rama away from home for a day's hunting in the forest.

As soon as Rama was gone Ravana leapt forward and with a terrifying 'R-o-a-r-r-r!' swept Sita up with his many arms. His evil plan was to fly back to Lanka and keep Sita a prisoner until she would agree to marry him. But Sita managed to take off her jewels and throw them down on the ground.

'I hope, I really hope, someone finds them,' Sita thought, 'and takes them to my husband Rama.'

Luckily, down below on the ground, the jewels landed just by Hanuman and Sugreeva.

'The gods must be sending us gifts!' said Hanuman.

'I wonder who these belong to?' asked Sugreeva.

The two set off into the forest to solve the mystery.

Meanwhile, prince Rama had returned and was calling for his wife Sita.

'Where has she gone?' he thought, as he searched the forest for her. Hanuman and Sugreeva found him wandering alone calling Sita's name.

'Who is Sita?' asked Hanuman.

'Sita is my wife, the princess,' said Rama. 'She has disappeared.'

'I see,' said Hanuman. 'Perhaps these jewels belong to her then.'

'Why, they are Sita's,' replied Rama. 'Where is she and who are you?'

'I am Hanuman and this is my king Sugreeva. We will help you find her.'

'Thank you,' replied Rama. 'Please do your very best.'

HANUMAN SEARCHES FOR SITA

Hanuman flew south. He learned that Sita had been taken to the city of Lanka by the demon king Ravana. Hanuman grew tall and mighty and with one giant leap began to fly through the clouds to the walled city on the island.

As he flew over the ocean his shadow was seen by a terrible sea monster.

'Grrrr!' she said. 'I'm very hungry and I'd like to eat you.'
She opened her mouth and swallowed him whole.

'Oh, Oh,' thought Hanuman, as he slid down her slippery throat.

Hanuman landed with a big THUMP! He was sitting on something soft. He looked down . . . he was sitting on a bed! Hanuman was floating inside the stomach of the sea monster! He peered through the darkness and saw bits of masts, bits of sail and ships that had been wrecked long ago. There were skeletons, giant fish and all sorts of things the sea monster had swallowed.

'I must get out of here,' thought Hanuman, looking around him. Then he had an idea.

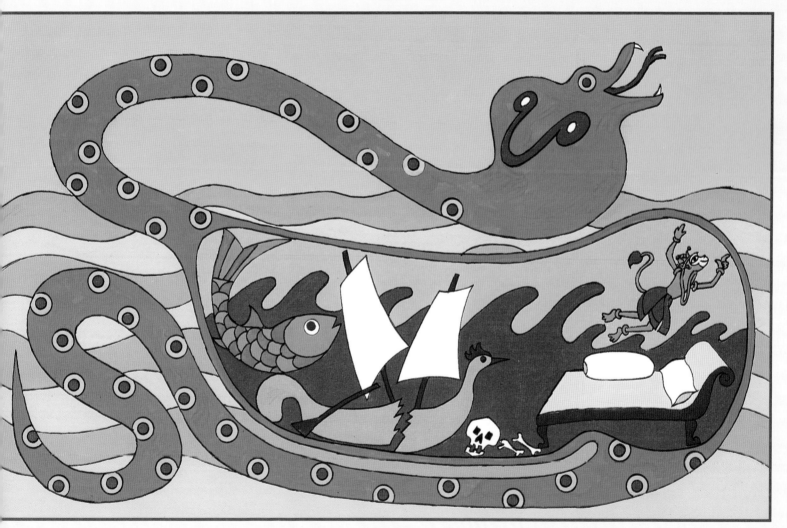

Hanuman made himself very small and flew around the monster's stomach tickling her sides. She began to squirm and thrash about.

'Hoo, hoo, ha ha! Stop that at once,' she giggled. 'I am very ticklish and if I laugh too much I'll sneeze!'

But Hanuman wouldn't stop. The sea monster could take it no longer.

'I think I'm going to . . .'

She opened her enormous mouth wide. All at once Hanuman shot out of her mouth.

'Ahh, Ahh . . . Choooo!' sneezed the sea monster.

She shut her great jaws suddenly as she remembered that Hanuman was supposed to be inside her. But he was already speeding away to the walled city of Lanka.

When Hanuman arrived at Lanka he saw all sorts of demon guards everywhere. Some were fat, some were thin. Some were beetroot red, some banana yellow and some were even cucumber green. All were ugly and smelly. They grunted as they walked around.

'Oh dear,' thought Hanuman, as he sat on the city wall.

He was still very small, so he managed to slip past the guards through the darkness without being noticed. Inside the white marble city he searched for Sita in all the rooms of Ravana's grand palace.

Hanuman searched in the dining hall. He searched in the kitchens. He looked down all the corridors. But he couldn't find Sita. Then he heard a great rumbling noise, like thunder, coming from a bedroom with a huge golden door. He quietly crawled under the gap in the door and found Ravana. He was fast asleep on a huge bed with all his ten heads snoring loudly.

'Grrrr–phew . . .Grrrr–phew!!'

'Well,' thought Hanuman, 'Sita certainly isn't here!'

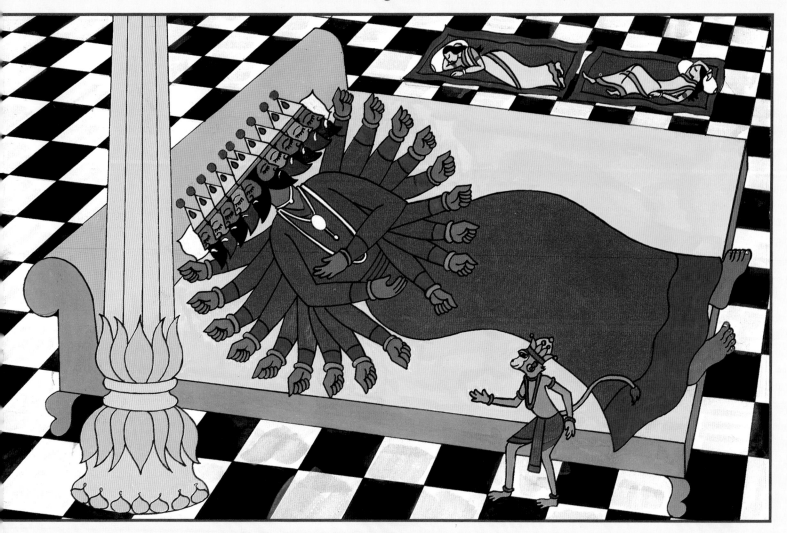

Hanuman found Sita outside the palace sitting sorrowfully in a beautiful garden surrounded by sleeping demons. He bent down from the branch of a fruit tree.

'Pssst!' he said, beckoning to her. Sita looked up in surprise.

'Who are you?' she asked.

'I am Hanuman,' he replied soft and low. 'I have been sent by Rama to find you. Now that I have I must return to tell him and we will come back and rescue you.'

'Oh, thank you!' Sita replied, cheering up a little. 'But be careful. Ravana is not only mighty but cunning.'

Just then one of the demon guards was disturbed and woke up.

'An intruder in our midst!' he shouted to the other guards. 'We must capture him!'

They raced to attack Hanuman, who suddenly made himself grow tall and strong again until he stood high above the garden. Reaching down towards the earth he pulled two trees with their roots out of the ground and swung them around like clubs to keep the demons away. When Ravana heard what Hanuman was doing he was furious. There was a deafening sound as his ten heads all roared and shouted at once.

'A monkey doing all this damage in my garden!' he cried. 'Send my son to capture him and bring him to me.'

Ravana's son went and began shooting deadly snake arrows at Hanuman, but they didn't harm the mighty monkey-man.

Fire!

Hanuman had a brilliant idea.

'Perhaps I should meet Ravana face to face,' he thought. Making himself small again he allowed himself to be caught. He was tied up and brought to Ravana.

'Please let Sita go!' begged Hanuman.

'Never!' snarled Ravana. 'How dare you! Set his tail on fire!' Several demons grabbed Hanuman's tail, but it suddenly began growing . . . longer and longer! It was knocking over the demons who could hardly hang on!

'Fools!' yelled Ravana. 'It's a trick! Grab his tail and set it alight!' Finally they managed to set the tip on fire and a mighty roar went up from the crowd. But the fire didn't hurt Hanuman at all because his magic powers kept him perfectly cool.

Hanuman's eyes twinkled as he had another idea.

'I know,' he thought. 'I can put my burning tail to good use!'
He suddenly grew big again, breaking free of his bonds. With one
bound he leapt into the air, his tail burning brightly. He looked like a
giant fireball! He then flew over the city of Lanka setting fire to the
roofs of the houses. Another roar went up from the demons, this time
in astonishment.

'Oh, how I hate that monkey!' Ravana stamped his feet and cursed
with rage.

He waved his twenty arms wildly, while Hanuman dipped his tail in
the sea.

'Sssssss . . .'

There was a loud sizzling noise, but Hanuman's tail was not burnt at
all!

Hanuman flew back to prince Rama to tell him what had happened.

'That's all very interesting,' Rama said, 'but how can we rescue Sita?'

'Don't worry,' said Hanuman. 'I have a whole army of monkeys and I will help you rescue Sita.'

They marched down to the southern tip of India where they were faced with the mighty ocean.

'How shall we cross?' asked Rama.

'My monkeys will build a bridge of rocks for you,' replied Hanuman. Using great stones and trees Hanuman and the monkeys built a strong bridge. Hanuman carried Rama on his shoulders and they crossed the sea to Lanka. The demon king Ravana sent his son to lead the demon soldiers. There they were, lying in wait and ready for battle.

THE GREAT BATTLE

What a fierce battle! Among the ugly, smelly demons and the poisoned spears and snake arrows, Rama fought bravely. Way up on the hillside Hanuman picked up rocks and hurled them. Then the demon king himself entered the battle. Ravana's twenty arms were here, there and everywhere, cutting, thrusting, and circling like a whirlwind. Every time one of Rama's arrows hit one of Ravana's heads, another would just pop up in its place! The demons moved forwards to attack Rama's army.

'This is no good,' said Rama to Hanuman. 'How will we rescue Sita now?'

'Hah!' sneered Ravana from afar. 'Foolish Hanuman. Foolish Rama – you'll never get Sita back now because *we're* going to win the battle!'

Hanuman flew close to Rama and whispered in his ear:

'Ravana's weak spot is his foot. There's only one sure way to kill him – with a magic arrow kept hidden in his own palace!'

Rama looked up. Hanuman was already flying away to Ravana's palace. Soon he returned with the magic arrow.

'Here you are,' he said to Rama. 'Let's hope this works.'

'It's our last chance,' said Rama, as he strung his bow.

Ravana was getting closer. Fire was coming out of his ten noses and smoke from his twenty ears. Rama took aim.

'Z–I–N–G!'

The arrow flew straight and sweet through the air. It hit Ravana's foot and he let out an ear-piercing scream. Then he fell, dying, to the earth.

Hanuman flew to Ravana's palace, freed Sita and returned her to Rama's waiting arms. They hugged each other.

'I missed you so much,' said Sita, 'but Hanuman gave me hope.'

'It is thanks to Hanuman that you are safe and sound,' said Rama.

'It was nothing really,' said Hanuman shyly, as he looked at the ground. 'Come on Sugreeva, we'd better be going now.'

'No wait,' replied Rama. 'You have done so much for us and we'd like to thank you.' Rama and Sita gave Hanuman and Sugreeva some jewels as gifts. 'From now on you will be our brothers. Please accept our friendship and join us.' Hanuman agreed. There was great rejoicing in the land. Hanuman lived happily ever after in the green forest and had many more exciting adventures.

This story is derived from the epic Hindu poem The Ramayana, which is over 4,000 years old. The poem forms much of the basis of Hindu religion and culture and the main characters are worshipped as gods and goddesses.

HANUMAN
(Hanoo-maan)
A demigod thought to be the ideal friend and hero, associated with strength, intelligence and magic.

INDRA
(Ind-ra)
Ruler of the Atmosphere and the Eastern Quarter of the Hemisphere, Indra also controls the weather.

RAMA
(Raam)
The reincarnation of the Hindu god Vishnu, Rama is central to The Ramayana. He symbolises holiness and goodness.

RAVANA
(Raa-van)
The ten-headed demon and cunning King of Lanka (now Sri Lanka).

SITA
(Seeta)
Worshipped as a goddess, Sita is considered to be a role model for many Indian women – beautiful, intelligent and devoted to her husband.

SUGREEVA
(Soo-greev)
The king of the monkeys, he is loyal and helpful. Hanuman leads his army and is his advisor.

VAYU
(Vai-yoo)
The god of the winds, Vayu controls the Northern Hemisphere and rides in a golden chariot drawn by 1,000 horses.

Published by BBC Books,
a division of BBC Enterprises Limited,
Woodlands, 80 Wood Lane, London W12 0TT
First published 1988
© Text by Rani and Jugnu Singh/BBC Enterprises Ltd 1988
© Illustrations BBC Enterprises Ltd 1988
The illustrations first appeared in the BBC Schools Radio programme *Let's Join In.*
Paperback ISBN: 0 563 21425 2
Hardback ISBN: 0 563 21426 0
Printed in Great Britain by Purnell Book Production Ltd.